Spectacles of Love
by Teresa Ives Lilly

Published by
Lovely Christian Romance Press
Copyright 2017 All Rights Reserved

Spectacles of Love

1890 MANHATTAN NY: CHAPTER ONE

Charlene Trumbel's hand shook slightly. It was the only indication of the anger she felt. Sitting at the end of the long table, listening to the conversation between her father and Mr. Robert Thornton had sparked her interest. However, the man's words upset her greatly. "Those in the lower class don't deserve help. They choose not to help themselves. They get what they deserve."

Charlene could hardly believe the man's words. Surely no one could possibly think that the thousands of poor people in New York *wanted* to live lives of poverty.

Just this week, her father read an article to her by a man named Jacob Riis called *How the Other Half Lives*. Using a new photographic method that ignited flash powder to provide enough illumination to take photos in darkness, Mr. Riis included photos of some of these poverty-stricken people. His hope in publishing the photos was to encourage the public to clean up the squalid conditions of the poor.

Why isn't father sharing the information from the article with everyone? I know he, too, believes in helping the poor.

As she sat, silently fuming, Charlene reached out for her water glass. Unfortunately, in the blur she could see, her hand missed the glass, knocking it over. The water began to spread across the silk tablecloth. The maid rushed forward, took the glass and pressed a clean cloth on the water to keep it from spreading.

"What a clumsy oaf you are." Charlene's stepmother, who sat beside her, leaned over and whispered through clenched teeth. "Is there no end to the humiliation I have to endure when you are present?"

Charlene's cheeks flushed. It was embarrassing for her as well as for her stepmother, but she couldn't help it. She was unable to see well.

Her private tutor suggested spectacles for her years earlier, but her father refused. Instead, he ended her education. And her stepmother, almost the same age as Charlene, wouldn't even consider it. Whenever Charlene even mentioned it, she would rage, "I'll not be seen with someone wearing spectacles. It's shameful. What will people think?"

Charlene was sure all eyes were on her, although she wasn't able to clearly see all the guests. However, a man's deep voice pulled any attention away from her.

"As you know, I'm a superintendent in Kansas at the West Side Lodging House for Homeless Boys. I also work as a placement agent under the director of the Children's Aid Society of the City of New York. I have seen firsthand the effects of poverty on the children of the poor."

Charlene recognized the voice of Mr. William J. McCully. She was glad to hear him speak up. He was an advocate for helping orphans in New York. In fact, under his directorship, several hundred orphans were sent to Kansas each year to be adopted by families in the West.

Robert Thornton interrupted the man. "Oh, no, McCully. Please don't start in with your 'Orphan Train' stories again. Haven't we all donated enough money to your cause already?"

Charlene gasped at the man's rudeness. She could never understand why her father allowed Mr. Thornton to step foot into their home. He didn't see things as she and her father did.

How I would love to speak out about this, her mind raged. However, she knew neither her father nor her stepmother would approve. Even at the age of twenty-four, already a spinster in her family's eyes, she still had to adhere to the childhood rules of being seen but not heard.

Yet her stepmother, just three years her senior, spoke quite as volubly as she wished about any and all subjects; about most of which, she knew nothing.

"Now Robert, Darling," her stepmother spoke to the man beside her in sweet, coy voice. "Let Mr. McCully speak. My dear husband, Charles, just dotes on him."

At that, all eyes turned to Mr. McCully, whose face showed a shocked expression. It was clear he did not need or want Mrs. Trumbel's protection from Thornton. Also, being a strict Presbyterian man, he didn't approve of the way Mrs. Trumbel's hand remained on Robert Thornton's sleeve.

He cleared his throat and continued, "Well, as I've said many times in the past, New York City is overrun with orphans. There is no place for them to go; orphanages and churches cannot take them all."

"So, do you believe we, the upper class, should take them in, preferably as servants?" one of the other guests asked. From the sound of her voice, Charlene suspected she was a member of the extremely wealthy Vanderbilt family.

"No. These children need clean air and invigorating work. That is why I became a Placement Agent for the Orphan Trains. We take as many children as we can out West. There are families willing to adopt these children or at least to take them on as foster children."

Thornton snorted, "More like slave labor, I'd say. However, it seems a better choice than allowing them to run wild in the streets of New York. They are sure to grow up to be thieves if left here."

Mr. McCully sighed. "If left on the streets of New York, more than likely they will die. Out West, some of the older children are put to work on farms, but the younger ones are often adopted into loving families. Reverend Charles Loring Brace, who started the Orphan Trains, developed what he called 'the family plan.' This means a child from New York, sent to Kansas or other states, can be taken into a home and treated as part of the family. Given the same food, clothing, education and spiritual training as their own children. "

"And what if they aren't given all those things, but are put to work instead?"

"He still believes these children have a better chance

at life out West than they have on the streets of New York. He has been sending groups since 1854."

"And what about you? How many children have you helped send West?" Charles Trumbel asked.

"Kansas alone has taken in over six hundred children to date, and I plan on sending more." The man spoke in a humble voice.

Charlene's respect for him grew.

"So now comes the begging for money," Thornton scoffed. "Every time you get a train full of those orphans gathered up, you come to those of us who have money."

Charlene wanted to reach across her stepmother and stick a roll into Mr. Thornton's mouth. The man was beyond rude. But Mr. McCully was not disturbed by the man's boorish behavior.

"Indeed, I do come to those of you who I believe can afford to help. If not you, then who?"

No one at the table seemed able to answer him.

Charlene's father spoke next. "McCully, we've all given to you in the past. Yet, this time seems different. I can see by the gleam in your eyes. Pray tell us what it is you need so we can go on with the meal."

Charlene covered her mouth to stifle a giggle. Her father did not like anything to interrupt his meals as his large waist indicated.

"Yes, thank you. Well, I was hoping you could sponsor this next group I'm sending to Kansas, Mr. Trumbel. Other wealthy men have been known to sponsor a group. The total cost for each child to travel to Kansas and to pay the Matron who travels with them is a mere ten dollars a child."

Charlene felt her stepmother stiffen beside her. "Charles! You can't possibly believe this to be the best use of your money."

Charlene noted the silence. She could imagine the look on her father's face. The man would give his new wife almost anything she asked for, but he would never abide being ridiculed or questioned in front of guests.

Mr. Trumbel's words came out from between pressed lips. "I'm sure you won't mind giving up a few new gowns this year, Dear. The price to help some needy orphans would be worth it. Don't you agree?"

"Yes... Yes, of course." Charlene could hear the tone of indignation in her stepmother's voice. But she knew the girl would never outwardly defy her husband.

"Good then. We would love to sponsor this next Orphan Train, McCully. When does it depart?"

"In two weeks. We are currently looking for someone to come along. The Matron we have scheduled has been recovering from a broken wrist. Although she will be able to travel, she will need help."

Charlene waited until all the guests left the table before she rose. When she could tell the others had left the room, she pushed back her chair and began to make her way around the table, holding onto the edge.

Although she could see well enough to maneuver the room, she was still apt to bump into other people or knock over things.

She shook her head sadly. *If only they would allow me to wear spectacles. My life could be so different. But they worry so about their public image.*

She stood and straightened her turquoise tea gown and smiled. *At least this is one thing that has changed. I'm no longer hampered by such tight corsets. The new invention of these looser fitting tea gowns has given me some freedom. I only wish I could wear them all day long, but for now, even if they can only be worn in the house, I'm happy to have some relief.*

As she made her way along the hall, she bit her bottom lip. Her father would expect her to come to the drawing room to mingle with his guests. Her stepmother, however, would rather she not be there at all.

I may be an old maid, but Stepmother cannot abide the fact that I'm pretty. Not that my beauty has ever won me any attention. The moment any man realizes I can't see very well, he turns away. Father can keep trying to foist me off on his friends, but I'm more apt to stay an old maid for the rest of my life.

With a slight bitter laugh, she moved more quickly. She wasn't sure who it would be worse to upset, her father or her Stepmother.

Stepmother won't like the idea of me continuing to live here with father for the rest of my life. I have to find something else to do, somewhere else to go.

Outside the drawing room door, Charlene shrugged her shoulders, took a deep breath and attempted to glide into the room. However, just a few steps in, she stumbled into a chair, which must have been moved by one of the guests.

"Oh!" she moaned, covering her mouth, trying to keep the gasp of pain quiet. She'd hit her knee rather hard on the chair.

Before she could even move, her stepmother was by her side.

"Again? I begin to believe you do these things just to get attention. Please refrain from such theatrics. Stand in the corner like a good daughter, and don't draw any more attention to yourself."

Charlene nodded and moved to the side of the room. She slid down onto a decorative chair and placed her hands in her lap. *It's going to be a long night.*

CHAPTER TWO

"Miss Trumbel, why are you hiding in this corner?" Charlene's thoughts were interrupted by Robert Thornton's voice.

She lifted her eyes to focus on his face. "I'm not hiding."

"Well, you aren't mingling."

"No, I'm not very good at socializing. I do better sitting quietly, listening."

Robert Thornton turned and pulled another chair across the floor and placed it beside Charlene. She was rather surprised.

"I hope you don't mind if I join you. I've heard enough from McCully for one evening."

Charlene swallowed, a sharp retort on her tongue.

"All that talk about orphans, as if they were his own children."

"Have you an objection to orphans?" Charlene asked, her tone sharp.

"Orphans? No, not in general, and I'm more than happy to know they are being toted out of New York. However, I do object to being forced to hear the stories about them."

"Hmm, I believe the best way for Mr. McCully to raise enough money, to 'tote' the orphans out of the city, is to raise awareness. What better way than to share stories about the children?"

Robert Thornton sat silent for a moment then, with a chuckle, said, "So I won't find any sympathy from you. You are a supporter of McCully then?"

Charlene crossed her arms and spoke through clenched teeth. "Yes, I am."

The man reached over and lifted Charlene's hand and pressed it to his lips. In irritation, she pulled away.

"Forgive me for being so boorish. I see my feelings about the Orphan Train have upset you. But may I make a solemn promise to you?"

"Me? What promise can you make to me?"

"The promise to sway my support to McCully and his Orphan Train project. I'm a wealthy man and can afford to support him, if that makes you happy."

Charlene felt confused. "I see no reason for you to be concerned about my happiness. I would have you support McCully from the kindness of your own heart."

"But, my dear, that is the point. I am concerned about your happiness. Haven't you noticed my recent increase in visits to your home and how I've made a point to seek you out for conversation?"

Charlene shook her head. "Indeed, not. I assumed you've been visiting your 'old friend,' my stepmother."

Mr. Thornton chuckled. "Altheia? She's a lovely creature, but, as you said, she is your stepmother. I'm not a man who is interested in married women. Now, someone younger, like you…"

Charlene's hand went to her throat. "But…" She was not able to go on because at that moment her stepmother stopped before them.

"What plan are you two hatching over here?" Her voice dripped with sarcasm.

Robert Thornton stood. "Plan?"

"Well, what else could have you both so absorbed?" Her eyes focused on Charlene.

Charlene could feel the woman's cold stare. She, too, stood. "I must say goodnight for the evening." She scooted along the wall and slipped into the hallway.

Oh Lord, I will never hear the end of this. Once Altheia discovers that Mr. Thornton is interested in me, she'll be very angry.

Charlene moved as quickly as she could to her room, avoiding the myriad of vases, tables and chairs that lined the hallway. Once there, she locked the door so there would be no chance of her stepmother entering her room until morning.

Soon enough to hear her complaints.

Charlene stepped across the room and pushed aside the curtains. The moon was full, lighting the entire evening sky. For Charlene, it was a blur.

Lord, You've blessed me all these years with a life of luxury and the love of my earthly father. I ask now for You to use me somehow to be a blessing to others and give me a way to leave this home and find love.

She pressed her head against the windowpane and allowed tears to flow down her cheeks.

The following morning, Charlene opened her eyes in surprise then laid still thinking of the dream from the night before.

Suddenly, it all became clear. The dream was not just a fanciful fleeting thing. It was an answer sent from God. She slipped off the bed onto her knees and bowed her head in reverence.

Thank you, Lord. It is all so clear now. I know exactly what to do.

Charlene dressed in her tulip bell skirt, which was snug and smooth over her hips but flared out to a wider hem, along with a lovely dark mauve blouse.

Although I can't see my own image clearly, I'm sure this outfit makes me look like a most sturdy woman. I'm sure Mr. McCully will not deny my wish.

When she stepped into the room for breakfast, her eyes fell on the long buffet set with several trays. There were many dishes to choose from, but she also knew that most of the food would go to waste.

Her father was already seated at the end of the long table. She quickly filled a plate and slipped into the seat beside him.

"Father, why don't we tell Cook not to make so much food? You know we never eat it all. It's wasteful."

Her father looked solemnly at her, then the corner of his eyes crinkled as he smiled. "Bent on saving the world today?"

"No, but have you ever thought about how many people have no food? Yet here we sit with more than enough."

"Yes, it often seems unfair. But keep in mind, I do work hard to pay for this food." His hand waved to indicate the buffet.

"Even more reason not to allow so much waste."

Her father took a bite of eggs then nodded. "I do think you're right. I'll have Altheia speak to Cook."

Charlene shook her head. "Best let me do it. Altheia may feel differently about it."

"Wise girl, I think you're right. Then I leave it up to you. Now, since we are talking about the squandering of wealth, I believe there is an article in the newspaper today to interest you."

"Really? What is it?"

"A man named Ward McAllister wrote a piece called *Opulence in the Gilded Age.* Seems to speak about wealthy families who live in unbridled influence. Describes a banquet given by some of our friends recently."

Charlene finished her breakfast then picked up the newspaper and began to read the article, holding it close to her face to see better.

"So, there you are!" Her stepmother's accusing voice pulled her eyes from the article. "I went to your room last night but found your door locked, and then I returned this morning to find your room empty."

Charlene set the paper down and looked up at the woman with innocent eyes. "Was there something you wanted to speak to me about?"

Altheia stamped a foot. "Yes, but first I don't think it's right for you to lock your door. This is your father's house, and he should have access to your room anytime he wishes."

Charlene turned to her father. "Have I ever denied you access to my room, Father?"

"No." He glared at his young wife. "What is all this about? If Charlene wants to lock her room, I see no reason she can't."

"Oooh. You always take her side. I don't know why I try to..."

"I'm sorry if you weren't able to speak to me," Charlene spoke gently, trying to stop the pending onslaught of accusations. "I was very tired and must have turned the lock by mistake. I'm here now. Was there something you wanted to talk to me about?"

Altheia filled a plate, overflowing with food, which Charlene knew the petite woman would not eat.

"I want to know what was going on between you and Robert."

"Robert? You mean Mr. Thornton? Nothing was going on. What do you mean?"

"I saw you and him with your heads together. It looked most cozy."

Charlene bristled. "It was nothing of the sort. We were merely speaking of the Orphan Trains."

Her stepmother gave her an accusatory stare. "I'm quite sure Robert would not have been speaking of anything so tedious. He doesn't approve of Mr. McCully always talking about the orphans. Why would he himself speak of them?"

"Perhaps he had a change of heart?" Charlene couldn't help but goad the woman. "He assured me he plans to sway his support to Mr. McCully."

Altheia sat down and nibbled at her food. "What would ever make him do that?"

"He promised to do it, to make me happy," Charlene spoke, immediately realizing she had just made a huge mistake.

"To make you happy? I can't imagine why Robert would care about your happiness. I insist you tell me the truth."

Charlene's father slammed his fist down on the table. Both women jumped slightly and stared at him.

"Altheia, enough! I happen to know the truth. Thornton has promised McCully his support. I heard him tell the man myself. And, while we are on the subject of Thornton, I'll advise you, my dear wife, to give up on keeping him in your entourage of admirers. He has switched allegiance from you to the young Charlene. In fact, he hinted to me before his departure last night that he'd be coming back to begin courting someone in my home."

Charlene couldn't see Altheia's features clearly, but she heard the woman's intake of breath.

Before her stepmother could say another word, Charlene pushed back her chair and stood.

"I'll go have a word with Cook, Father. Then I plan to run down to the Children's Aid Society Building and speak to Mr. McCully about trying to help."

Her father sat up. "I'm not too sure I like the idea of you going there. It's not the best part of town."

"I'll have our driver take me right to the front door. I'm sure it will be fine." Charlene turned and walked determinedly out of the room. The last thing she heard was her stepmother's whining voice asking, "Why is she going to speak to Cook?"

Charlene sat in the carriage staring out the window as the driver weaved his way across town. She could feel herself fuming with anger. She wasn't sure if she were angrier about Altheia and her accusations or with Mr. Robert Thornton, who had somehow given the impression he planned to begin courting Charlene.

Not that I haven't always wished for a handsome man to court me. But, Lord, Thornton is the complete opposite of the type of man I would want. He and I see nothing the same.

Charlene watched fuzzily as a horse-drawn omnibus passed by. Her father was a supporter for the newer use of small steam locomotives called "dummies" to pull streetcars. She wondered, however, if it would be a good idea. *Could horse-drawn carriages and steam locomotives work together on the tight streets of Manhattan?*

From her seat in the carriage, she saw the storefronts, each with a striped awning over the sidewalks. The buildings, each at least three stories high, were also apartments for those who lived in the area.

Just then her driver stopped the carriage. Charlene slipped her head out the window to see why.

"Sorry, Miss," the driver called back. "Had to stop or run into a group of street urchins."

"Are they gone now?" she asked.

"Yes, Miss." The driver clicked the reins, and the horse began to move again.

Charlene sat back with a frown. Suddenly she felt the carriage dip slightly in the back. She squinted her eyes trying to see out the small window. What she was able to see was the back of a young man's head. One of the street urchins must have jumped on the carriage.

At first, she wanted to call out for the driver to stop and deal with him, but she quickly realized the boy meant no harm.

I won't deprive him of his fun, she decided.

Charlene kept looking out the window. Finally, the boy turned his head, his eyes opened wide in surprise when he noted her watching him.

"Good afternoon," she called through the window.

She could see the look on the boy's face. He was trying to decide if jumping off was his best option.

"Please don't jump off. I'd hate for you to get hurt. I don't mind that you've hitched a ride."

The boy's face lit up with a smile. "Mighty kind of you, Miss."

"When we stop, please don't run away. I'd like to speak to you."

The boy's eyes grew wary.

"You needn't worry. I'll not call the police. In fact, I'll pay you for your time."

"Pay? Alright then." The boy seemed appeased.

Finally, the carriage came to a stop. The driver jumped down and opened the door. Charlene stepped out and moved to the back. The boy was there, swinging his legs.

"Miss, shall I call the police?" the driver asked, seeing the child. The boy looked ready to bolt, but Charlene reached out and placed a hand on his arm.

"No. This young man has agreed to allow me to interview him."

The driver gave an odd stare.

"Interview?" the boy and driver asked in unison.

"Yes. I plan on writing an article for the newspaper about different people I meet in the city. You are my first."

The boy's eyes bulged.

"But first, I have a meeting in this building. Will you come along and wait for me?"

The boy's eyes traveled to the building. He tilted his head and asked, "What kind of place is this?"

"It's the Children's Aid Society Building. Can't you read the sign?" She pointed at the plaque above the door.

The boy kicked at a loose pebble and mumbled, "Can't read."

"Oh, I see," Charlene answered, as if it were a regular affair of her life to meet a person who couldn't read. "Can I persuade you to come with me? You may sit out in the hall and wait for me until my meeting is over. Then, perhaps I could take you for an ice cream soda?"

She could see that sparked some interest in the boy's eyes.

"What about money? You said you'd pay me."

The driver took a step toward the boy with a raised hand. "The cheek. You hooligan, how dare you..."

Charlene turned and held up her hand to stop the driver.

"James. I appreciate your gallantries, but I am in no need of protection. Please come back in a half hour for me."

She spoke with authority, held out a hand and waited. The boy stared at her for a moment then placed his dirty palm into her hand.

CHAPTER THREE

Charlene walked down the hallway and stopped outside the office door. There was a chair sitting there. She looked down at the boy beside her. "What is your name?"

"Andy."

"Okay, Andy. Will you sit here and wait for me?"

The boy's eyes scanned the area. He shrugged and sat. "Sure, but someone'll come along and kick me out."

"Not here they won't."

The boy didn't look convinced, but Charlene promised to return quickly. She opened the door and stepped into the office. A clerk looked up.

"May I help you?"

"Yes, I would like to speak to someone who is in charge of the Orphan Train project."

"Hmm, well, Mrs. Alden is usually who you would speak to, but she's away at the moment. We do have Mr. McCully here today."

Charlene wanted to clap her hands. "That would be fine. He knows who I am. Just tell him that Miss Charlene Trumbel would like to speak to him."

The clerk stood and disappeared into another office but returned only seconds later.

"Mr. McCully will be glad to see you." She held the door open and indicated for Charlene to enter.

"Oh, there's a young boy out in the hallway. He is with me. I was wondering if you might have something he could eat."

The clerk walked over, opened the outer door and looked at the boy.

She turned with a nod. "I'll take him something." She smiled.

Charlene proceeded into the room. Mr. McCully stood up.

"Miss Trumbel, what a pleasure. Have a seat. How can I help you?"

Charlene stood still and tried to focus her eyes. Most of the room was blurry, but she was able to make out the larger items and moved to a chair and sat gingerly on the edge.

"I'm glad you're here, Mr. McCully, because you are the person to whom I actually wanted to speak."

The man tilted his head slightly. "About what?"

"The Orphan Train."

"Oh, my favorite subject. But may I ask why?"

"I'm considering trying to write an article about it for the newspaper. To tell the truth. Perhaps make the wealthy families in New York understand the need for it and try to get you more support."

Mr. McCully was quiet for a moment. "Do you really want to know the truth? How far are you willing to go to find out the truth?"

Charlene swallowed. "I'm not sure what you mean."

"I mean, are you willing to ride the Orphan Train? To learn firsthand how the entire process works?"

Charlene felt a bit stunned by the thought but slowly nodded. "Yes, I am."

"Perhaps you heard me mention we needed someone to ride along with our Matron on the next train. If you went along, you would see how the whole thing works."

Charlene looked slightly shocked.

"You can even meet the children beforehand."

"How long would I be gone?"

"A few weeks."

Charlene's hands grew sweaty. Fear gripped her chest, but the memory of her stepmother's constant criticism flashed through her mind.

"I'll do it."

Mr. McCully stood and moved around to the front of the desk. He reached down and lifted her hand. "My Dear, you have no idea how much this will mean to us here at the Children's Aid Society. But do you believe your father will allow this?"

Charlene felt her hope crash. Her father would not approve. But she would just have to convince him.

"I'm sure it will be fine. What will I need? What should I do?"

"If you can meet me at the orphanage tomorrow afternoon, you can meet the Matron. She will be able to answer all of your questions."

Charlene agreed, stood and shook hands with Mr. McCully. He didn't let go of her hand at first but leaned closer.

"Miss Trumbel, I'm a bit concerned. I noticed the other evening, you squinted and stumbled several times. Are you in need of spectacles?"

Charlene blushed. "Oh, I'm fine. I was a bit tired the other evening. That's all."

McCully smiled. "Good, because the children can be a handful and need to have a sharp eye kept on them."

Charlene left the office feeling flustered. She was excited about going on the train with the orphans, but Mr. McCully's concern about her sight niggled the back of her mind.

I've gotten along fine all these years, Lord. Surely, a train ride with some children shouldn't be a problem.

She purposely pushed the lie she'd told to the back of her mind, but it kept creeping out. Finally, she stamped her foot.

I was tired the other night so that wasn't a lie.

As she made her way across the outer office, she ran right into a small trashcan beside the clerk's desk. She tried to convince herself that anyone would have bumped into it, but she knew, deep within, it was because she couldn't see it.

When she opened the outer door, Andy stood up.

"The lady in there brought me some cookies and a sandwich. Pretty good eats."

Charlene giggled at his words then sobered picturing the sideboard of wasted food she picked at this morning.

"Andy, do you have a family? A home?"

"No."

Charlene stared at him in perplexity. "Then where do you stay?"

The boy hesitated then mumbled, "I have a box."

"A box?"

He nodded and stared back at her innocently.

Charlene wasn't sure what else to say. The idea of living in a box made no sense to her.

She held out a hand for the boy. "Come with me."

The boy moved beside her, a wary look in his eyes. "You promised me some money."

"Yes, but I think we need to get you a real meal first."

They stepped out of the building; Charlene stopped on the front stoop.

"Andy, do you see the carriage I came in?"

The boy looked up at her curiously. "It's right in front of us, Miss."

"Wonderful, come along." She sallied forward. When they reached the street, James was standing by the carriage with the door opened."

"Get in the carriage, Andy."

"What!" Both James and Andy again spoke at the same time. James finished with, "Miss, I don't think…"

"Thank you for your thoughts, James. But I would like Andy to come to the house with me. I'm sure Cook can provide him a decent meal."

James stiffened.

Andy took a step back, but Charlene grasped his arm. "Remember you promised to let me interview you."

"Interview?" Andy asked, and Charlene realized he had no idea what the word meant.

"I want you to tell me about yourself so I can write an article for the newspaper."

"Cor, Miss. What would you want to know about me that anyone else would want to read about?"

Charlene assured him he would be a big help if he came along with her. Andy was reluctant, but a ride in a carriage was too tempting for him to pass.

When they reached home, Charlene and Andy got out of the carriage. She turned to go in the front door, but James spoke up.

"Miss, wouldn't it be better if I were to take, uhm, your guest to the back entrance?"

Charlene could hear the disapproval in the man's voice.

"No, Andy will join me." She took the boy's hand again and led him into the house.

Once inside the foyer, Andy stopped and gave a low whistle.

"Some place, Miss."

"Thank you, Andy. It belongs to my father. Come along; we can go to the parlor. I'll have the maid bring you a plate, overflowing with 'good eats.' Then we can get started on that interview."

As they walked down the hall, suddenly Charlene stumbled. If it hadn't been for Andy's quick movement, she may have fallen.

"Didn't you see the bucket there, Miss? Looks like someone's been mopping the floors."

"I must have been looking the other way. I'm glad you caught me. How strong you are! How old are you?"

Andy gazed at Charlene a moment then shrugged. "Don't know."

"You don't know your age?"

"Nope, neither does Dale or Joe. We's all been together for as long as we can remember."

"Are you brothers?"

"We don't think so. Least ways, none of us looks like the others. But we looks out for one another."

They reached the parlor and turned into the room. Charlene told Andy to sit on the sofa, but he watched as she carefully reached out in front of herself, feeling for the back of the sofa.

"Miss, ain't my business, but truth be told, you can't see a bleedin' thing."

Charlene took in a short breath.

Andy went on. "I can see you don't want anyone to know it so I won't be blabbin'."

Charlene sunk onto the sofa with a sigh. "Thank you, Andy. It's not something we speak of."

The maid came into the parlor, and Charlene ordered a tray of sandwiches and cakes. She couldn't see the girl's reaction but could imagine the shock on the young maid's face at seeing the street urchin.

"Now," Charlene smiled. "You asked earlier why anyone would want to read about you. Well, perhaps people wouldn't want to read about you, but I want them to read about you. I want them to know all about what life for an orphan in New York City is like. Perhaps it will change some of them. Make them give more money to groups like the Children's Aid Society and the Orphan Trains.

The boy cocked his head slightly. "What's an Orphan Train?

Charlene explained the Orphan Train to Andy, and his eyes lit up at her words.

"You mean, the kids who ride that train gets a family?"

She hesitated. She couldn't say that for sure. "Most of them. I've been told that some of the older children are often hired to work on the farms."

Andy sat back and crossed his arms as if to indicate his lack of interest. But, suddenly he sat up. "And, you're going to go on that Orphan Train to help?"

Charlene nodded.

Andy frowned. "Guess I better go along with you. You don't know enough about orphans. You'd have your hands full, and besides..." his voice dropped lower, "you might need some help getting around."

Charlene leaned forward until she could focus on Andy's dirty face. She bent over and kissed his forehead.

"Thank you, Andy. I'd love to have you along with me. After we eat, I'm going to have the maid take you to the kitchen. The staff will find you some new clothes, get you a bath and give you plenty more 'good eats.' That is, if you will stay here until the Orphan Train leaves the city?"

Andy nodded slowly. "Dale and Joe will wonder where I've gone."

"Can we stop by and see them tomorrow? I want to go to the orphanage and meet the Matron."

"Sure, I've been gone overnight a few times. They won't worry. I only wish they could be here, to get some of this here food."

"I'll have Cook pack a big basket full. We can take it to them."

Andy tilted his head and gazed at the woman with a look of adoration and mumbled, "Thank you, Miss."

CHAPTER FOUR

The following day, Charlene and Andy climbed back into the carriage, ignoring the look on James' face. It wasn't long before the carriage drew up in front of the orphanage.

"Do your friends live near here?" Charlene asked.

Andy nodded. "Just down the alley over there." He pointed further down the street.

"Shall we meet the Matron first, then go see them?"

Andy agreed and walked beside Charlene, guiding her past any obstacles she might not see.

At the office, Charlene asked Andy to wait outside. He slipped onto a chair while she went into the office.

A stout, grim faced woman sat behind a desk. Her wrist in a cast. "May I help you?"

"My name is Charlene Trumbel. Mr. McCully told me to come meet the Matron for the Orphan Train.

"I am the Matron. My name is Miss Ranton, but you may refer to me as Matron. Mr. McCully informed me you would stop by." She sat silently staring at Charlene then said, "We appreciate your offer to help, but are you sure about this? Traveling across country with twenty-five orphans can be difficult."

Charlene sat up straight. "I'm sure I can be a help."

The woman shuffled several papers. Then sighed. "I'm sorry. It's difficult for me to admit I need help. I appreciate your offer."

Charlene relaxed. "Mr. McCully said you would tell me all about the Orphan Train."

The woman nodded then pushed a flyer across the desk. "This is the notice we send out to newspapers in the towns where the train will stop." Luckily, the words were large enough for Charlene to read.

"Homes Wanted for Orphans"

"We usually have one male and one female agent accompany each group, but this time Mr. McCully cannot travel with us. With my broken wrist, there are things I will need help with."

"I understand. And what about the orphans. Are they excited?"

The Matron cleared her throat. "We feel it's best not to tell the children about the trip until the night before departure. Then they are bathed, given new clean clothing and have their hair tended to."

Charlene thought it strange the children weren't given more notice.

"You must think that seems harsh, but some of the children believe their parents will return to the orphanage to get them. However, in most cases, it isn't true. We feel it's best not to tell them about being placed on the Orphan Train beforehand because some of them might try to run away. It would be worse for them to end up on the streets."

Charlene swallowed. It did sound harsh, but if she were to go on this journey, there would be many new ideas she must accept.

"When we reach the different towns, I will need you to help prepare the children, line them up and help escort them to the places the towns have set up for them to meet prospective parents."

"What type of places?" Charlene was very intrigued by what the Matron was telling her.

"Some towns have us go to the local opera house, sometimes the town hall, or a church. We line them up on a stage or platform at the front of the room. Usually a local town committee has been at work prior to the arrival of the train, trying to line up good potential families for the expected children.

"These people and other members of the community are allowed to visit with the children. If a family wants a certain child, and we believe it to be a good match, then the child will leave the group and go on to their 'new home.'"

Charlene tried to imagine the entire process.

"So, do you still want to go along? The train is crowded, uncomfortable and dirty."

"Yes, I've made a commitment to Mr. McCully. By the way, I met a young boy recently. He's an orphan, but I've taken him in. I would like him to travel along with me."

"Will we try to place him?" The Matron didn't sound pleased.

"No, I think he'll want to stay with me. However, if the opportunity presents itself, and he wants to go with a family, will that be alright?"

The Matron sniffed. "What type of boy is he?"

"He's in the hallway, waiting for me. Would you like to meet him?"

The Matron stood and moved around the room. She opened the door slightly and glanced out. Then returned to the desk.

"He seems healthy. We only take healthy children. He's older; more than likely he'd be offered farm work, not necessarily a family."

Charlene nodded. "I understand, and I would leave the decision up to him."

The Matron gave Charlene a bit more information and asked if she could meet them at the train station an hour before departure.

"You don't want me to meet the children a few days before?"

"It's not necessary. You will have plenty of time to get to know them on the train ride."

Charlene agreed and stood to leave. The Matron walked ahead of her and opened the door. "Then, we shall see you. If you change your mind, let us know as soon as possible so we can find someone else to help."

Charlene understood the woman's apprehension and doubts.

She probably sees me as the spoiled daughter of a wealthy man, who wants to pretend to help just for attention. However, I shall prove myself invaluable to her.

"Are you ready to go, Andy?" She held out a hand for the boy.

He stood and scuffed a foot on the ground. "Miss, I think it would be better if you stay in the carriage, and I just give the food to the gang."

"But, why? I want to meet your friends."

"It's not a very nice place. It's dirty, and there's bound to be a rat or two."

Tears pressed at the back of Charlene's eyes, thinking of the life Andy lived.

"Thank you, Andy, but it's time I see the truth for myself."

When they reached the carriage, Charlene asked James to hand the basket of food out to her. As she and Andy began to move away from the carriage, James stepped up and stopped them.

"Miss Trumbel, where are you going?" His eyes scanned the area ahead.

"Andy and I are taking this basket of food to some of his friends."

"I can't let you do that. What would your father say?"

"James, Father doesn't need to know about this. The boys live in that alley, right down the street."

"I best come along then, Miss."

Charlene could feel Andy bristle beside her. "She don't need you. I can take care of her. 'Sides, if anyone sees you, they'll hightail it out of there."

James glared at the boy.

"Please, James. If you must, you may walk us to the end of the alley, but I insist you not follow us any further."

"Very good, Miss." James took a step back and followed behind Charlene and Andy.

Andy looked over his shoulder several times at the stiff man. "He don't like me, Miss."

Charlene gave his hand a small squeeze. "Don't worry. That's just the way he acts. Most of the time, I think he doesn't like me, but I know it's not true. He's one of the most faithful people I know."

The alley was dirty and smelled of urine and other various dank odors. Charlene kept her head straight ahead, grasping onto Andy's hand as hard as she could.

"Bit further, Miss." Andy steered her.

As they moved into the alley, Andy began to whistle. However, Charlene realized it wasn't a song; it was a pattern.

"Are you sending your friends a message?"

"Yes, Miss. That way they knows it's not the coppers. There's Joe now, just stood up."

In the murky distance, Charlene could make out the shape of a small person.

"Hello, Joe. Got a friend here, and food!" They reached the other boy.

"Whatcha bringin' her here for?" Joe's surly voice asked.

"She wanted to give you a basket of food. Course, if you don't want it, then we can leave." Andy taunted the other boy. Charlene held out the basket.

Joe's hand stuck out, and he grasped the basket, pulled it from her hands and opened it. The boy gasped. "Andy, this is more food than I've ever seen. It'll last us weeks."

Andy shook his head. "Not me, Joe. I'm going away soon, at least for a while."

Joe pulled out a roll and began to tear into it.

"Whatcha mean? Where you gonna go?"

"This here is Miss Trumbel. I'm going on the train to a place called Kansas with her. Gonna help her take care of a bunch of orphans."

Joe sat on a wooden box. "Whatcha wanna do that for?"

Charlene spoke. "Andy's coming to help me because I don't see very well."

"Well, Andy's always helpin' someone. He found this alley for Dale and me. But things is looking up a bit cause we both got jobs selling papers. Starting next week."

Charlene was glad to hear it. She had been tempted to ask Joe to come along on the Orphan Train, but she doubted the Matron would accept another street urchin.

Joe stopped chewing long enough to give a whistle. "You got on new clothes, Andy?"

"Yes, the Miss here gave them to me. And for now, I'm sleepin' in a real bed."

Charlene cringed. The small bed, in the attic room of her house, could hardly be called a real bed. Until she returned from Kansas, however, she didn't want to upset her stepmother by insisting on a room for Andy.

Oh, Lord. What will I do once I return from Kansas? I'm sure writing an article about the Orphan Train will not pay enough for me to be able to afford a small home for Andy and me.

Andy slapped his legs. "We gotta go now, Miss. Joe, you tell Dale good-bye for me."

"Sure, Andy."

Charlene and the boy turned and slowly made their way back to the street. James was standing at the corner, a worried expression on his face.

Andy smiled up at him. "Here she is, safe and sound. I won't let nothin' bad happen to her."

James didn't smile, but he did reach over and swish his hand over the boy's hair. Charlene knew they'd made a bond.

James helped her into the carriage; Andy hopped in beside her. In seconds, they were headed away from the only home Andy had ever known.

After several minutes, Charlene realized the boy was strangely silent.

"Will you miss it?" she asked.

Andy wiped his arm over his eyes. "Not the alley, but Joe and Dale been my best friends. I guess I'll miss them some."

"When we return from Kansas, we can come visit them again." She tried to soothe the boy, but he pushed away and shook his head.

"They won't be there. When they start earning money, they'll find something a bit better. Won't be much but might be a real building."

Charlene was quiet, allowing the boy his private feelings. She wanted to cry for Andy, and for Joe and Dale, but she knew that wouldn't help. Instead she began to think of how she would put this all in her article.

CHAPTER FIVE

When Charlene explained to her father her plan to ride the Orphan Train and help the Matron, the man pounded his hand on the table, but Altheia comforted him and encouraged Charlene. "Dear, she's a grown woman. This will be a wonderful adventure for her."

Charlene knew the woman only supported the idea because she wanted Charlene out of the house, even if only for a few weeks. After much grumbling, her father wagged his head and said no more.

The next few days, Altheia was helpful, even offering to go with Charlene to shop for appropriate traveling clothes, but Charlene was content with what she owned.

"A sturdy skirt or two with several blouses should be all I'll need. I won't be going out into society."

So Altheia left her to her own packing and made plans to host several "Tea Parties" while Charlene was away. The guest lists not surprisingly included some very handsome young men.

So far, Altheia had not learned of Andy's presence, which suited Charlene. Each day she had James pick her up in the carriage, and Andy would already be there. They would travel into the city, where Charlene could observe what life for orphans on the streets was like. Andy was able to point out which children were orphans and how they were trying to survive, even though she wasn't able to spot the pickpockets.

As their departure drew closer, she grew more restless. The home she'd grown up in, with all its luxuries, felt stifling. She yearned for something different. To be able to live a life with meaning.

Finally, the morning of the departure arrived. She said her farewells the evening before so she and Andy slipped out early in the morning. James drove them to the New York Grand Central Terminal, where they found the Matron and a group of twenty terrified children. There were also five babies, under ten months of age.

Andy had become Charlene's eyes and told her in accurate detail what she could not see. Before she even got out of the carriage, she knew how many boys and girls there were and an idea of their ages.

"The Matron doesn't look very happy," Andy mumbled.

Charlene and Andy got out of the carriage, said a private goodbye to James, then moved down the platform to greet the Matron. James carried the suitcases behind, set them down, then reluctantly left the train station.

"Good morning, Matron." Charlene tried to keep her voice from quivering.

"I was beginning to wonder if you were coming after all." The Matron's stiff back showed her irritation.

"I'm sorry if I'm late. I'm here now and ready to begin work. You remember Andy?"

The Matron didn't acknowledge the boy's presence.

"I want you to meet the children. Introduce yourself to each of them so they will know who you are. Once we get on the train, the children need to be seated and kept quiet."

Charlene nodded. She turned with Andy at her side, steering her with his hand.

When she reached the group of children, she began to introduce herself to each of them. There were five boys older than Andy. They didn't seem interested in anything but the train. The five older girls had already been assigned babies to care for; they weren't interested in meeting Charlene either.

The last group consisted of six boys and four girls between three and ten years old. The youngest was a charming little girl who still sucked her thumb.

As the children responded to her friendly voice, she could hear nervousness in theirs. One boy named John asked why he couldn't just go back to the orphanage. "My Mam might come looking for me today."

Charlene wasn't sure what to say. She asked the Matron if the children knew where they were going.

"No, we didn't have time to tell them last night. For now, let it just be an adventure. Once we are all boarded and, on our way, you can explain it all to them."

Charlene was shocked to think these children had no idea what was happening to them.

Finally, the train pulled into the station. For a moment, the air was filled with thick black smoke, and the sound of the squealing brakes was frightful.

Minutes later, the Matron told Charlene it was time to get the children on board.

Charlene tried to raise her voice loud enough to be heard over the crowded platform, giving instructions for the children to line up and board the train. Andy ran up and down the line, demanding the children's attention. Finally, he grasped Charlene's hand.

"Everyone is ready to go. You just turn around, and we can lead them to the train."

"Thank you, Andy. I'm sure I would be lost without you."

Charlene climbed the two large steps and turned right to enter the compartment where she and the children would be. Andy was behind her and wasn't able to stop her from bumping into a large suitcase sitting on the floor by the door.

"Ouch." She stopped and leaned over to see the offending item.

"I'm sorry, Miss." A man's gentle voice spoke quite near her ear. Charlene straightened so quickly the man didn't have time to pull back, and she knocked her head into his chin.

"Umph."

"Ouch." She exclaimed again.

"I am sorry, Miss." The man's words were muffled as he held a hand over his chin and mouth.

Charlene tried to focus on the man's face. He was tall with dark hair.

"I'm sorry. It was clumsy of me to knock into the case."

"I shouldn't have left it in the walkway. I'm always leaving my things about. It's a bad habit I have."

"Perhaps your wife better remind you, in the future." Charlene spoke in a somewhat teasing manner.

"Indeed, if I had a wife, she would probably help keep me in line. Alas, I have no wife."

Charlene giggled at the obvious joking tone.

The man looked over her shoulder. "Seems we are blocking the way for your children." He sounded surprised. "Are these all your children?"

"No, these are all orphans."

"Orphans?"

"Yes, have you heard of Orphan Trains?"

"No."

"Well, I can't tell you about it right now; I need to get the children on board."

"Perhaps later. I just realized I'm in the wrong compartment and need to find the correct one, but I'd love to come back and hear all about it."

Andy pushed up in front of Charlene and stood with his hands on his hips, glaring at the man. "Can you let us by?"

The man stepped to the side, lifted his case and moved out of the compartment.

Charlene felt her cheeks turning red. She was embarrassed by Andy's behavior. But she moved further into the compartment so the children could all enter.

She leaned over and whispered, "Andy, we need to be polite to people on the train."

"Hmph, I saw the way he was gawking at you." Andy answered with a sneer.

"I'm sure he was doing no such thing. Now, take the little ones to the front seats and help them get settled in."

Andy pressed by her, and the group of children followed him. Charlene could already feel a bead of sweat trickle down her spine. The train compartment was cramped. The seats were hard wood. It promised to be an uncomfortable trip.

Then she remembered the man stating he would come back to talk to her about the Orphan Train. She couldn't help but duck her head to hide a smile.

An hour later, the children were all staring out the train windows as the locomotive made its way out of the city. The children called to one another, pointing at things they'd never seen before. Whenever a child asked Charlene about the sites, Andy would hush them with a stern look. He'd quickly risen to leader of the group. Even Charlene felt he was more capable than she.

"Miss Trumbel?" The Matron's voice interrupted Charlene's thoughts.

"Yes?" Charlene looked up.

"I believe it's time to tell the children a bit about what will be happening the next few days. I find it makes things smoother to tell the children on the train before they reach the first town."

The Matron moved to the front of the compartment and clapped her hands. The children all sat up straight, with their hands in their laps.

Just before the Matron began to speak, Charlene felt the presence of a person hovering beside her. She turned and glanced up. It was the same man she'd bumped into earlier.

"I've come back to hear about the Orphan Train."

Charlene felt her cheeks warm. "Sit here, beside me. The Matron is about to explain things to the children."

Charlene scooted closer to the window, and the man sat beside her.

"My name is Bronson Jacobs, by the way."

"Hello, Mr. Jacobs. My name is Charlene Trumbel."

The man grabbed her hand, pressed it into his and gave a small shake. "I'm very pleased to meet you, Miss Trumbel."

Charlene nodded then turned her attention to the front of the compartment.

"Children," the Matron began. "I'm sure you are all wondering why you were brought to ride on the train today. The reason is because there are people in towns out West who want to take in boys and girls from the city."

Charlene could hear the murmurs around her. But the Matron clapped again, and the train car was silent.

"There aren't many people in the city who want to take in children or adopt older children so we at the orphanage have agreed to send you to these towns. When we reach each stop, you will be taken to a building, and the people who are interested in adopting a child will be there to meet you all."

"I don't want to be adopted. My Mam's coming for me any day." The same boy Charlene met earlier spoke.

The Matron clapped again.

"I know a few of you have parents who are living. But your parents are not able to take care of you."

Charlene noted the man beside her fold his arms over his chest. *He doesn't like the whole thing,* she thought.

"But families in the West will be able to take care of you. They will give you food, send you to school and to church."

"I'm too old for school," one of the older boys stated.

"Yes, Carl, that's true. You older children will probably be asked to work on farms, instead of being adopted. Even so, it's a better life than you would have in the orphanage or on the streets."

The group of children was silent. Charlene could sense their worry.

"When we reach a town, Miss Trumbel and I will help you all freshen up, get in a line and go to the building. When the people come to meet you, be nice, smile and speak up if they ask you a question. The best way to get chosen for a family is to let them see how smart and sweet you are."

Some of the older boys laughed. "Guess I'd better just show them how strong I am," the oldest one stated.

"All of you will be taken to towns in the state of Kansas. We have to transfer trains twice before then. It will be a day or so before we reach the first town.

The Matron finished speaking and made her way back to her seat. When she moved past Charlene's seat and noted the man sitting there, she frowned.

Bronson leaned over. "Is everything she said true?"

Charlene nodded. "Yes."

"And, what's your part in all of this?"

"I came along as a helper. I plan to write an article about the Orphan Train for the newspaper. To show the wealthy families in Manhattan why they need to support the Orphan Trains."

"Hmm, I guess I see some benefit in the whole thing."

"Yes, the cities are too crowded. The orphanages are not very nice places for a child to grow up. The hope is that the children will get to live in the country where they will be healthier overall."

"What if the person who adopts the child isn't very nice? I have several neighbors who would jump at a chance to get free labor but wouldn't treat the children very well."

"I was told the Matron checks on all of the children in the first year. If they're unhappy, they can go back to the orphanage or try another family."

"I see."

Andy stood up and stepped closer to Charlene's seat. His brows drew together when he saw the man sitting beside her.

"I believe your young bodyguard isn't very happy to see me sitting here."

"Yes, he has taken his job very seriously. He was living on the streets, in a cardboard box, with two other boys. He has agreed to come along and help me on this trip."

"Will he be adopted out, too?"

Andy overheard the conversation then spoke up. "No, Sir. I'm here to help Miss."

"What about when the journey ends? What will become of young Andy?"

"He'll come home with me." Charlene assured the man.

"And do what? Be trained as a butler, or a driver?"

Charlene felt herself grow defensive. "Either would be a good job."

"Yes, but do you really believe he will ever fit the requirements? I think you do him an injustice."

"What do you mean?"

Bronson stood and stretched. "What I mean is, Andy has a better chance for a good life in Kansas than he has returning to New York. Just think about it."

Bronson moved away. Charlene watched his fuzzy form disappear. Andy sat down in the now empty space beside her.

"What's that guy want to be buggin' you for?"

"He was interested in knowing about the Orphan Train."

"What's he care?"

Charlene patted the boy's arm. "Andy, I'm sure Mr. Jacobs has his reasons for being interested. I'm glad you came along to help me, but I must insist you try to be pleasant to everyone, including Mr. Jacobs."

Andy crossed his arms.

Charlene sat quietly for a time, thinking over what Mr. Jacobs said to her. She agreed that Andy would probably never be able to become a butler or a driver. Perhaps a footman, but she bit her bottom lip trying to picture that. Even with years of training, the boy wouldn't fit into a household like her father's.

"Andy, I'm wondering if you'd like to get a family in Kansas. You could work on a farm. You might like it."

"I came along to help you, Miss. I got no plans to get adopted or hired out. But, you don't have to worry about me. When we get back to New York, I can find my own way. There's always the newspaper."

Charlene gasped slightly. "I didn't mean anything, Andy. Of course, you won't leave me when we get home. I've promised you a home."

"How come you don't get married?"

Charlene leaned close to him. "You know about my sight. Men don't want to marry a woman who is always bumping into things."

Andy stared at her, a bit surprised. "But, Miss. You're a pretty good-lookin' doll. Most men would be happy to get a good looker."

Charlene laughed. "Not the men I know. But I appreciate the compliment."

Andy sat for a long time thinking. He'd come along to help Miss Charlene, but she was going to need something more. She needed a husband.

The image of the tall, strong looking man, Mr. Jacobs, suddenly came to his mind.

Andy turned back to Charlene. "Where does that Mr. Jacobs live? What does he do?"

"I'm not sure. I didn't ask him those questions. It wouldn't be proper."

Andy sat back again with a huff. Proper or not, he was going to find out all about the man.

CHAPTER SIX

After transferring several times, they were finally on the train that would take them to Kansas. The Matron told Charlene the names of the towns where the train would stop. Washington, Fredonia, Elk City, Independence and finally Cherryvale. Charlene thought the last one sounded nice.

A few miles outside of Washington, Kansas, the Matron informed the children they would be making their first stop soon. Charlene passed a basket around with sandwiches and apples. The children gobbled the food down. The Matron assured her that other meals would be provided by the towns they stopped in, but not this first one.

"Now, children. We need to make sure all of you look your best. So, we will wipe faces and comb hair."

Charlene asked Andy to line the children up by her so she could see each of them and help them with their grooming. She whispered encouraging words to them.

"Them babies will go first," Andy stated. "Families always want babies."

"Yes, I think you're right. But there will be other families looking for older children as well."

When she finished with the last child, a deep voice spoke. "Is there anything I can do to help?"

Charlene turned in surprise. "Mr. Jacobs! I didn't realize you transferred to this train."

"Yes, I'm heading home."

"Oh, where's that?" Charlene felt her cheeks blush at the forward question.

"I live in Cherryvale, Kansas."

Andy overheard their conversation and slid up beside the tall man.

"Miss Charlene likes that name."

"I'm glad to hear it. Perhaps, Miss Charlene will allow me to show her around the town?"

Charlene cleared her throat. "I doubt that will be possible. As soon as the children are presented and chosen, we will board the train and head back to New York."

"Sit down and tell Miss Charlene all about it." Andy pressed.

Charlene shook her head. "Andy, I'm sure Mr. Jacobs has other things to do."

"Not at all. But The train is pulling into the station. I thought I'd come along; see how this whole Orphan Train selection process works. I'd love to tell you about Cherryvale later."

"That would be nice," Charlene agreed. She could feel her heart beating a bit more rapidly.

Suddenly, the wheels began to screech, and the train slowed. Black soot filled the air outside the train windows. The children sat with their noses pressed to the windows, but they were all silent.

When the train stopped, the Matron told Charlene to get the children off the train and line them up. She would find the place where the children could meet prospective parents.

Charlene made the announcement to the children. She suggested the older girls carry the babies and the others line up from youngest to oldest behind them.

The children scrambled to get into order. Several of them didn't know their exact age so Charlene had to fit them in where she thought they belonged.

"I don't want to go," the young boy named John insisted.

"I tell you, my Mam's gonna come and get me any day now. She won't know where I am if I go with some family."

Charlene hugged him and whispered. "I promise we will let your mother know where you are."

The boy's eyes filled with tears.

Bronson stooped down and gave him a small, light chuck on the chin.

"I think your mother would be proud to know you're getting a chance to live on a farm and to grow up big and strong."

The boy looked up at the tall man and wiped his tears. "You think so?"

"I know so. If she was having trouble taking care of you in the city, she would want to know you are being cared for in the country. Even if she can't take care of you right now, it will make her happier to know you are getting good food and clean air."

The boy seemed mollified and straightened his shoulders. Bronson moved down the aisle and gave several words of encouragement to the other children who seemed exceptionally worried.

He's a good man, Lord, Charlene thought. *Nothing like the men I've met in New York.*

"I like him," Andy stated, which surprised Charlene since Andy didn't like Mr. Jacobs at first. "I think you should marry him."

Charlene's head swung around, and she placed her hands akimbo on her hips. "Andy, don't ever let me hear you say anything so ridiculous again."

"What'd I say wrong?"

"Mr. Jacobs is a nice man, traveling on the same train as we are. That doesn't mean…" She was so flustered by his comment; she wasn't even sure what to say to him. "Just… don't say it again."

"Okay, okay. It's time to get off the train."

Charlene nodded and made her way up the aisle to the front.

"Children, follow along now. We don't want anyone getting lost."

They all trooped off the train, Andy in the lead, following the Matron who'd returned. Charlene was next with the orphans behind her. Mr. Jacobs hung back but traipsed after the group.

Charlene grasped Andy's hand. The Matron was no more than a blur in front of her. Although Washington,

Kansas, wasn't a busy city like New York, Charlene felt overwhelmed.

Andy kept quietly calling out the obstacles for Charlene. "Loose board two steps ahead; move to your right. Watch out for those barrels on your left."

"I'm so grateful you are with me. I shouldn't have come. I've gotten so used to my own home and getting around; I didn't realize just how bad my eyesight is."

They finally stopped. Andy stepped closer to Charlene. The Matron clapped her hands, and the children all stopped and turned, giving her their full attention.

"The town has invited us to use their church. We will enter, and you will all line up on the stage. Remember to smile and speak up when someone asks you a question."

The Matron opened the door, and they all began to enter. As soon as the older girls carrying the babies stepped through the doors, several women rushed over.

"I want a baby!" Each of them yelled and tried to pry the infants from the girls' hands.

Charlene was pushed out of the way; she would have fallen if Mr. Jacobs, who had somehow slipped up behind her, hadn't caught her.

"Goodness," she gasped. "What should I do?"

The man told her he would take care of things. He turned around and in a deep, loud voice, called for silence and attention.

Once it was quiet, Charlene instructed the girls to carry the babies onto the stage.

She assured the women they would all get a chance to see the babies.

The children all lined up on the stage, except Andy. He stood faithfully beside Charlene.

"Andy, I know you want to help me, but I want you to consider trying to get adopted. It would be a better life."

Andy turned away and whistled to himself, pretending he hadn't heard her.

Mr. Jacobs was standing on Charlene's opposite side. She thanked him for helping.

"I'm used to ordering people around. I own a brick factory in Cherryvale, and I oversee most of the work."

"That sounds interesting."

"Hmm, yes, I suppose it is. I've been doing it so long, I believe I've lost some interest."

Charlene squinted, trying to see what was happening on the stage. It looked as if there were many adults speaking to the various children.

"I hope the children all find good homes," Bronson said.

"I've been praying for each of them. I believe God will work things out."

"I appreciate a woman with faith. I've been praying for the children as well."

Charlene smiled. She'd never actually heard a man speak about God before, except the minister at her church, of course.

"Andy, get closer and let me know if there's any trouble up there."

Andy frowned. "You sure?"

"Yes. You can be my eyes."

Andy nodded and headed for the stage. After a few minutes, he returned.

"Well?" Charlene said.

Andy stood rigid beside her.

"Andy, what's wrong."

"I was only up there a minute. Some old farmer came over, grabbed my mouth and tried to look at my teeth."

Charlene covered a giggle. "What did you do?"

"I bit his hand."

Bronson slapped his leg and laughed. "That ought to teach him to tell the difference between a horse and boy."

"Mr. Jacobs, please don't encourage him. Andy needs to learn the right way of behaving."

Bronson gazed at her lovely face. "I tell you what. I'll agree to your wishes if you'll agree to call me by my first name, Bronson."

Charlene wasn't sure what to do or say. In New York, she would not have used a man's first name until they'd known one another months. She did understand, however, in the West, things were different.

"Alright, Bronson, and you can call me Charlene. But you must uphold your end of the bargain."

"I promise. As a matter of fact, I'll start right now. Come along, Andy. You and I will go up on the stage together and make sure the farmers don't treat the children like horses. Let's hurry, I think someone is looking at Dan right now." The man turned to move.

Andy brightened, but then he shook his head. "I'll stay here with Miss Charlene."

"No, Andy. Go along. I'll be fine."

"Are you sure?"

"I'm positive."

"Okay, then." He turned and followed Bronson.

Charlene waited a few minutes but wanted to see how things were going. She took a few steps, trying to get closer to the stage.

"Umph." Once again, she found herself kneeling over and pressing her bruised leg. This time, it was a small stool she'd tripped over.

"Let me help you up," Bronson's voice called her attention away from the ache in her leg.

She allowed him to take her hand and pull her to a standing position.

Charlene smoothed her dress. "How clumsy I must seem to you. First tripping over your suitcase and now this stool."

"No, I don't believe you are clumsy. It's obvious that you are in need of spectacles. Do you own a pair and just refuse to wear them due to vanity?"

Charlene coiled back as if slapped, but before she could answer, their conversation was interrupted by the Matron.

"Miss Trumbel, can you please escort the children from the stage now? Those who have been chosen by families are already in line to fill out the paperwork. Just lead the rest back to the train."

Charlene nodded and once more cautiously made her way to the stage. This time, Andy met her and walked beside her.

"Children, can you all follow us back to the train now?" Charlene pulled the children's attention away from the line of families who had chosen a child to adopt.

The group fell in line easily and quietly followed as Charlene and Andy led the way. Once again, Bronson brought up the rear.

"Are there any babies left?" Charlene asked Andy.

"Nope, poor things almost got torn apart by those women. Ten of 'em wanted babies."

"Did any of them take older children?"

"A few, but for most, it was a baby or nothing. The Matron told them she would be back in a few months with another group of orphans."

Charlene shook her head. It seemed to her, if a woman wanted a child, age wouldn't matter.

CHAPTER SEVEN

The children were strangely quiet. Each one slipped into a seat on the train and sat without saying a word. After several minutes, Charlene heard a few snuffles and realized some of the children were crying.

She walked down the aisle and stopped to speak to each child. All the babies were gone, and four others.

"Deena, why are you crying?" Charlene sat beside the seven-year-old and pulled her into a hug.

"I thought that nice lady who smelled like candy was going to take me home. But then she picked Carol 'cause Carol's younger than me."

"I'm sorry. I think God must have a better plan for you. That woman must have been who God wanted for Carol."

"Maybe..."

"I'm sure. I'll be praying you get the right family."

"I'd like to have a baby sister. My Ma had a baby girl; she only lived a few days. I wanted to take care of her, but everyone told me I was too young. After she died, Ma brought me to the orphanage."

Charlene swallowed the lump in her throat.

"You're a brave girl. A family will be lucky to have you."

After a few more minutes, Charlene stood and moved on. Just then, Bronson entered the compartment. He immediately noted the boys who were on the verge of crying. He made his way over to them and began talking to them. She was sure he was giving them the comfort they needed.

Finally, after speaking to all of the children, Charlene collapsed into her seat. Andy sat down beside her.

"I'm sure glad I wasn't one of the orphans up on stage today."

"Why?"

"Well, besides getting angry about people checking my teeth, I would've been mad if I wasn't chosen. These kids are all scared they won't get chosen. They figure if they don't get a family or get hired out, then the orphanage will toss them out."

Charlene shook her head. "No, that won't happen."

"It will for the older boys. The orphanage won't keep them once they turn sixteen."

Charlene looked surprised. "How do you know?"

"Oh, Ron over there, the oldest boy. He's fifteen. He told me. But he's been in the orphanage for so long, I'm not sure he could make it out on the streets in New York."

Just then Charlene heard someone clear his throat. She looked up. It was Bronson.

"I couldn't help but overhear what Andy just said. I believe it is true. Several of the older boys spoke of it."

"Oh, I thought the older boys would be the most reluctant to get adopted or hired out."

"Perhaps they felt that way at first. I'm going back to my compartment. Is there anything I can do for you before I leave?"

Charlene remembered his earlier words about her eyesight. "No, thank you. We are capable." Her voice sounded tight.

Bronson moved away.

"Why you being so mean to him?" Andy asked. "You told me we needed to be polite."

She hung her head slightly. Her behavior wasn't very Christian like. She'd been embarrassed when he noted her need for spectacles.

"You're right. I was rude. I'm just tired; it was a long day. I hope we can all get some sleep tonight before we reach the next town."

Andy agreed.

The following morning, the train slowed again and stopped in the town of Fredonia. The children were not as excited this time. Most of them either feared not getting chosen, or getting chosen for the wrong reason.

"If anyone tries to check my teeth, I'm going to punch them," Carl, one of the older boys, declared.

Abby, a ten-year-old girl, sidled up to Charlene and whispered, "If a family wants me, do I have to go with them?"

"That's the idea. If you aren't comfortable with it, just wave for me, and I'll come. Then we can talk about it."

"I want to be part of a big family. Before Ma and Pa got the fever, they promised there was gonna be more kids."

Charlene hugged her. "We can pray and hope for the perfect family for you."

When the train stopped, Charlene once more made the children get in line. Their hair was combed. The children each wore a similar looking outfit, which the orphanage had provided, so they would look clean and attractive.

Before they got off the train, Charlene found one girl pressed against the corner of her seat. She was crying.

"What's wrong, Susan?"

"I miss my brother," the girl sniffed.

"Your brother?"

"Yes, they wouldn't let him come with me. He's kind of sickly."

Just then, the Matron walked passed. "Miss Trumbel, why isn't Susan in line?"

"She seems concerned about her brother. She says that he was left behind?"

"Yes. He wasn't healthy. We only send healthy children on the trains."

Charlene stepped away from Susan and lowered her voice. "But surely they could have been adopted together?"

"Hardly. It is rare a family will take two children. Most brothers and sisters are parted during these trips. It's actually easier that Susan left him behind at the orphanage. She at least will know where he is and can write to him. If he were on the train, they might be adopted out to different families, in different towns, and never see one another again."

Charlene stared at the woman in horror. Then, finally gulped and nodded, "I see." She turned back and encouraged Susan to join the other children. She promised if Susan were adopted, she would give the family the orphanage address so she could write to her brother.

In Fredonia, the Matron led the group to an opera house. There the children were lined up on the stage and the prospective families began to look them over.

This time, Charlene stood on stage, listening to the questions the people asked the children. There were a few which caused her anger to rise, especially those farmers looking for free workhands.

Andy stayed close to Charlene.

"There's Mr. Jacobs. He just came in with a couple."

Charlene squinted but then dropped her eyes. She didn't want to appear to be interested. However, Bronson joined her on the stage, the couple not far behind.

Bronson spoke. "Charlene, I want you to meet Mr. and Mrs. Peterson."

Charlene turned, a bit surprised. "Hello."

The couple smiled.

"The Petersons had a young son, who tragically passed away several years ago."

"I'm so sorry for your loss."

"I thought... well, do you think they'd be a good match for John?"

The couple looked at Charlene eagerly.

Charlene hesitated. "John believes his mother is coming back to the orphanage to get him. I'm not sure he will be very agreeable to going with anyone."

"Yes, at first. But I believe they will dote on him and take such good care of him, after a time, he may accept the facts better than if he were to end up somewhere, shall we say, less comfortable."

Mrs. Peterson stepped forward, "Bronson told us about John. We agreed to come meet him, but if he really doesn't want to go with us, we understand."

"Did you plan to adopt a child today?" Charlene asked.

"No, we are Bronson's friends. When the train arrived in town, he sought us out and told us about John. That's why we are here."

Charlene smiled at Bronson. "That was kind of you. I think you should take them over and introduce them to John. You did promise him a nice life on a farm."

Bronson led the couple across the stage, and they all sat down with the boy.

"That Bronson sure is a nice guy," Andy's words interrupted her own similar thoughts.

"Miss, you better go see Abby. She looks upset."

Charlene allowed Andy to lead her to the girl. There was a haggard looking woman standing beside her.

"Is there a problem?" Charlene asked. Abby slipped behind Charlene.

"I want this girl, but she says she won't come with me."

Charlene didn't like the looks of the woman.

"I told her I need a strong girl. I own a nice laundry business in town. I'd even pay her a bit. But she keeps saying no. Is she allowed to do that?"

"I'm sorry, but yes she is. We usually hope the children will be happy with their placements." Charlene knew she was telling a falsehood, but she couldn't help herself.

"Aside from that, we are looking for homes for these children. Would you allow her to attend school and church?"

"Shucks, no. I need a worker. I'd feed her good though."

"I'm sorry, but no, she cannot go with you then."

Just then, the girl standing beside Abby spoke up. "I'm fourteen. I'm strong. I don't need to go to school. I'm willing to come and work for you if you promise to pay me."

The woman turned her eyes away from Abby, and she and the girl quickly slipped off the stage.

Charlene wanted to interfere again, but Andy grabbed her hand and pulled her away.

"But, Andy. That woman is awful."

"No, you don't have to worry. That's Carla. She's only been at the orphanage a year. I knew her when she lived on the streets. She's tough. She can handle that woman, and she'll be happy to get good food and money."

"Are you sure?" Charlene bit her bottom lip.

"Yep. She wouldn't like living on a farm. She'll be happier in town."

Charlene sighed and allowed the girl to be led to the adoption table with the gruff woman.

Just then, Bronson and the Petersons walked up to Charlene. Mrs. Peterson was holding John's hand.

"It looks like we've found a nice place for John," Bronson stated.

Charlene glanced down at the small boy. He smiled shyly. "Just 'til Mam can take care of me."

Charlene bent over and gathered the boy in her arms. "I'm so glad. They seem like a nice couple."

John whispered in her ear. "They're sad 'cause they had a boy who died. I'm gonna try and make 'em happy again."

Charlene kissed him and watched as the new little family walked away.

When she stood, Bronson was still standing there. "That was very kind, Bronson."

"I've been trying to figure out a way to help them get over their grief. That's part of why I was so interested in the Orphan Train."

Charlene cocked her head. "Any other reason?"

"Because of you." His voice lowered.

"Me? Why because of me?"

Bronson didn't get a chance to answer because the Matron clapped her hands and the children, still on the stage, quietly lined up beside Charlene.

Charlene squinted, trying to count the children, but she couldn't see clearly past the sixth one.

Bronson frowned. "I'll meet you on the train." He stalked away.

Charlene wondered what had upset him.

She and Andy led the children to the train, where they were given a boxed lunch provided by the town.

The train wasn't scheduled to leave right away, but Charlene wondered if Bronson got back on or not. However, a few minutes later, she saw his large frame fill the doorway.

He took time to speak with each child again. This time there weren't any tears, but a few of the children did feel rather let down.

Charlene was glad Susan had been adopted by a pleasant looking couple who promised to let her write to her younger brother. They even hinted about trying to send for him once he was well.

"That was a nice town," Paul, a twelve-year-old boy stated. "I wanted to stay there."

Bronson ruffled his hair. "Elk City is next. That's a nice place, too. There is a sawmill, a brick yard, a wagon factory, and another factory that makes bed springs."

The boy's mouth gaped open in awe.

"But, I'd rather see all of you living outside of the cities, on farms."

"I've never seen a farm. What they got on farms?" another boy asked.

"Hmm, cows and chickens, horses and pigs. Lots of land to run around on. Fresh air…"

"What's a cow?" one girl asked.

"What's a pig look like?" another boy asked.

Bronson wasn't sure how to answer. He moved closer to Charlene.

"They've never seen books with these animals in them. Remember, these children live in an orphanage," she whispered.

Bronson nodded again then turned and rushed off the train.

"What'd you say to him?" Andy asked, in a rather accusatory voice.

Charlene sat up straight. "I didn't say anything to him."

"Why'd he run off then? What if he misses the train?"

"I'm sure I don't know. He is an adult, and I'm certain he won't miss the train."

Andy stared out the window, worry etched across his brow. Finally, just as the train began to puff and move, Bronson jumped back on the steps and entered the compartment.

He held up a book and shouted, "I've got a book here with pictures of farm animals."

The children all clustered around him, but he made them all return to their seats, promising that once the train got moving he would come around and show everyone the pictures.

The children all sat, but their eyes followed Bronson. Even Andy kept his eyes glued to the book in the man's hand.

CHAPTER EIGHT

When the train stopped in Elk City, Charlene moaned inside. She was tired of sitting on the hard bench seats, and sleeping on them was even worse. She longed to take a brisk walk, but in these strange towns, she couldn't risk falling over things.

Since seeing the picture book about farms, all the children were excited to be adopted. Charlene could hardly keep them from jumping off the train.

The Matron once more went ahead to find out where the prospective families would be. When she returned, she wasn't very happy.

Miss Trumbel, please only line up the children ten and older."

Charlene was taken aback. "But, why?"

The newspaper ad was printed wrong. It specifically stated the children we were bringing were all older than ten. So, there are a small handful of farmers looking for helpers."

"Goodness. Are you sure we should take any of the children then?"

The Matron straightened. "Yes. The older children have been told that farmers would probably take them to work. Please line them up."

Charlene stood in front of the compartment of children and explained what happened. "So, for now, you younger children will stay here on the train. I expect you all to sit in your seats quietly until we return."

Heads nodded, but the room was quiet.

The older children stood and moved into line. Charlene could feel their excitement.

Andy followed the Matron; Charlene followed Andy.

As soon as they reached the building and got the children on stage, Charlene sent Andy back to watch the little ones. She was a bit surprised not to see Bronson.

There were several farmers looking over the children, but Charlene was worried about Abby. She'd been able to keep the girl from being adopted out at the previous town, but she wasn't sure she would have much say today.

Charlene stood near Abby and watched. The farmers passed her by. They were looking for boys. Each time she was passed up, Charlene let out a small breath.

Finally, a woman and man stepped in front of Abby. They asked her several questions. Abby answered quietly. Charlene stepped closer and listened.

The woman turned and pointed at a row of four young children sitting on the front row. "Those are my little ones. I told my husband he could get a boy to help on the farm if I could get a girl to help me."

Abby glanced at the children. "Will I be allowed to go to school and church?"

"Yes. I'm not looking for someone to do all the work. I just need an extra pair of eyes to help me with the little ones. They are always getting into mischief, and I've got another due in a few months."

Abby's eyes fell to the woman's protruding stomach, and her own eyes lit up.

"I'd like to come with you. I've always wanted to be part of a big family." The woman's eyes crinkled. She smiled and took Abby's hand.

Charlene was glad to see the father had selected Paul as well. She wondered if they would have enough room for so many children. She stepped forward to ask.

"Yes, Miss. We have a big home, with lots of room. We knew we wanted to have a whole passel of children so we built a big enough house first."

Charlene accepted the statement and gave Abby a goodbye hug. She was glad God found the girl a large family.

When the family left the stage, Charlene sighed. *I won't ever have a family of my own, Lord, all because I can't see well.*

Just then, the Matron called for Charlene. The girl made her way carefully down the steps.

"Yes, Matron?"

"Miss Trumbel, it has come to my attention that you misled us."

Charlene cocked her head. "In what way?"

"You assured Mr. McCully you could see just fine. But, it's not true, is it?"

Charlene's hands clenched. "No, it's not. But Andy has been helping me."

"That's not good enough. I can't take such a risk. Here is Mr. Jacobs. He has agreed to take you to meet a friend of his who sells spectacles. I don't see why you haven't gotten any before this, but if you want to continue on the trip with us, I insist you get a pair. I'm sure your father can afford them."

"But my father doesn't want me to wear spectacles."

The Matron's lips formed a grim line. "You needn't worry about that. I will speak to him when we get back to New York and explain why I insisted on them. For now, go with Mr. Jacobs and take care of this."

The Matron turned and stalked out of the building with the remaining children following. Four had been taken by the farmers.

Charlene stood alone, wondering what to do. She didn't know where she should go.

"Charlene?" Bronson's voice startled her. She turned around. "I hope you aren't upset with me for speaking to the Matron about your sight."

"I am upset. You had no right to interfere. Andy and I were doing fine. Now I can't continue the trip."

"You can if you get spectacles."

"Yes, but my father doesn't approve of them. Nor does my stepmother."

Bronson reached out and lifted her hand. "Your parents don't understand what you are going through. Believe me, wearing spectacles will make your life so much nicer. If you don't want to wear them in front of your parents, don't."

Charlene's shoulders sagged. "I have no choice now. I can't make it back to New York alone, and to continue with the Orphan Train, I'll have to get spectacles."

Bronson tucked her arm in the crook of his. "Just lean on me, and I'll lead you. My friend owns a general store in town, but they have a nice selection of spectacles. I'm sure we can find something for you."

Charlene moved her feet, but her mind rebelled against the man's highhandedness. When they reached the general store, Bronson opened the door and led her in. The room was not well lit so Charlene could hardly see anything at all.

Bronson called out, "Mason, this here's the lady I was telling you about."

Charlene's head shot up. "You talked to him about me?"

"Yes. I didn't mean any harm. I just want to help you."

Charlene bit her lip to hold back her anger.

Bronson guided her through the overstocked store to a table with a large glass case full of spectacles. "Just try them on 'til you find some." Bronson handed her a pair, which she fumbled, trying to slip on. There was no difference. She shook her head and handed them back. Bronson gave her another pair.

After six tries, Charlene was feeling frantic.

Lord, what if none of them work? What will I do? How will I get back home?

Bronson must have noted her agitation. "Charlene, don't worry. We will find you some that work."

He handed another pair to her, and she slipped them on. What happened then was unbelievable. Suddenly, the counter she was looking at grew clear. She could see the details of all the spectacles in front of her.

"Oh, my!" Her voice fluttered. She looked up and turned around and around. She could see the entire room. She could read the signs, which indicted the prices of items, with no problem.

Finally, her eyes rested on Bronson. She took two steps back. He was alarmingly handsome, with wavy brown hair and green eyes.

"You can see?" Bronson asked.

Charlene nodded. Her eyes filled, then tears began to slip down her cheeks. She brushed at them. "I don't know why I'm crying."

Bronson pulled her into his arms and pressed a kiss on her forehead. "Because you're experiencing a true miracle—one of God's very own. He gave man the wisdom to create these spectacles."

"I can't believe it."

Bronson smiled. "Let's set those to the side and try on the rest. We want to make sure we get the best pair."

Charlene didn't want to let them go, but she did.

"I don't see how anything could be better."

But, to her surprise, the final pair she put on made things even clearer than the others.

Suddenly Charlene gasped. "I don't have any money to buy these. The Matron didn't give me money."

"I'll take care of it."

"I'll send you the money once I talk with my father. He'll understand that it's a debt."

"Do you want to wear them now?" He handed them to her, and she slipped them on.

"Yes, it's just too good to be true. To be able to see where I'm going, without needing help. I know I was angry at you, Bronson, but now all I can say is, thank you!"

CHAPTER NINE

When they left the general store, the sun was bright, and Charlene felt slightly unsteady.

"It will take some getting used to," Bronson assured her. He slipped her arm in his again, and for the first time in her life, Charlene strolled down a street without bumping into anything.

At the train, Bronson helped her up the steps, as a gentleman would do, not as someone who was giving aid to an invalid.

She stepped into the compartment and could clearly see all the children. At first, they were busy talking, but one by one, they turned and noticed her.

The group grew quiet, all of them staring at her spectacles. Andy moved forward, a frown furrowed his brow. "You got spectacles?"

"Yes, Mr. Bronson helped me pick them out. I can see everything now." She reached over and hugged Andy. "I can see what a handsome young man you are."

The boy's shoulders sagged. "Guess you don't need me now." He scuffed his toe.

Charlene leaned over and whispered, "I may not need you to guide me, but I still need you. I've come to trust your judgment with the other children. And besides, you are coming home with me, aren't you?"

Andy shrugged. "You sure you still want me?"

"Yes. I'll always want you. The only reason I would be willing to give you up is if you find a family on this trip you want to go with."

The boy's head shook back and forth. "I'd rather stay with you."

"Good, then it's all settled."

The others asked questions about her spectacles. She allowed the children to hold them and look through them.

"I can't see a thing; they make everything blurry," one girl stated.

"That's because you can see. But for me, they make things clear. I've never been able to see anything unless I held it close to my face. Now I can see all the wonderful sites out the window as we travel to the next town."

Just then, the train began to move. Charlene got the children all quieted and then slipped into a window seat and pressed her nose against the glass.

As the train pulled away from the town, she was able to see the long, tall, swaying Kansas grass that seemed to go on for miles and miles.

From time to time, there was a farmhouse in the distance, and she wondered what it would be like to live in such an isolated place.

"Penny for your thoughts?" She turned when Bronson spoke, a huge grin on her face.

"I'm having a marvelous time, just seeing things."

"But, there's nothing out there but fields."

"Well, I've never seen a field before. Look at the flowers and the sky; it's all so beautiful."

"Just like you," Bronson lowered his voice.

Charlene raised her face and stared at him. "How can you say that? I mean, with these spectacles, I'm sure I'm not very attractive."

"What makes you say that? At least now you aren't squinting. That was not very attractive. I believe your spectacles are charming."

Charlene didn't say anymore; she was sure he was just being kind. Her parents had made it clear that people who wore spectacles were not attractive.

He's such a gentleman.

Bronson moved around the compartment, speaking to the children left on the train.

Charlene relaxed, thinking about all the things she would like to do now that she could see. However, she knew her parents would object to her wearing the spectacles.

I wish I could live on my own, Lord. Now that I can see, I could take care of myself. I don't think writing for the newspaper will turn into a career. At least not in New York.

Bronson returned and sat beside her.

"Bronson, do women in Kansas ever live alone, or are they all married?"

"Hmm, most of them are married, but a few women run their own businesses. It usually only happens if their husbands die."

Charlene sunk back. "Oh."

"Why do you ask?"

"It's just… I don't want to live with my parents. I love them, but I want a place of my own. Now that I can see, I'm sure I could find a way to make a living. But I believe they would be appalled if I tried to work in New York. I was wondering if I could find a job in Kansas."

"There isn't anything in Independence, but Cherryvale might have options. Let me think on it. Can you cook?"

Charlene nodded. "Yes, our cook often taught me. It will be so much easier now."

"Can you sew?"

"Not very well. But actually, I think now that I can see, that may change. At least I'll try."

"Do you want to be a writer? Isn't that what you told me you were doing on this train? We do have three newspapers in Cherryvale."

"That would be a dream come true, but would they hire a woman? I have no formal training."

"We can always ask. You remember, I live in Cherryvale so I'll do anything I can to help you."

Charlene's cheeks turned a pink hue. "I'm sure you have family and friends who need your attention."

"Not really. I keep to myself. I know just about everyone in town, but I have no immediate family, and I don't socialize often. My business keeps me busy. I'd be very happy if you would settle in Cherryvale." He lifted her hand to his lips and pressed a kiss on it.

"What about me?" Andy, who must have been standing nearby and overheard their conversation, interrupted them.

Charlene looked up at him. "Would you consider staying with me, in Cherryvale?"

A myriad of feelings swept over the boy's face.

"But, I understand if you want to go back to New York. I did promise to take you back."

"Would I get to live with you if you stay in Cherryvale?"

"Of course."

Bronson inserted a comment. "In Kansas, you could be more like a son to Miss Charlene; whereas in New York, you would have to work in the house as a servant."

"Do you want me to be your son?" Andy's voice trembled.

Charlene's head bobbed up and down. "Yes. I've always dreamed of having children. You could go to school…"

Andy frowned, and Bronson laughed.

"It won't be so bad. I think you'll like it. I'll help you." He turned and gazed at Charlene. "It's settled then. We'll try to find you a job in Cherryvale!"

The train stopped in Independence, and the children were lined up on a small stage inside a saloon. The Matron kept clucking her tongue in disapproval. There were six children left, and they were all nervous.

Charlene happily moved from child to child, assuring them they would all find homes.

The Matron acknowledged her spectacles with a nod.

Independence was a smaller town, but four children were selected. Carl and Pete, two of the older boys, were chosen by farmers. Mary, an older girl, was adopted, and a family with two younger children adopted Deena. She was happy to have a younger sister. All the children seemed pleased with their prospective placements.

The only two remaining were Donald and Denver. They were brothers, who were eight and nine. Up to now, the Matron allowed them to pass up being separated, but she did tell them if they weren't chosen before the last town, they would have to accept being split up.

Charlene was about to gather the two boys and head back to the train, but Bronson suggested a picnic at a nearby river.

The Matron agreed since the train was not scheduled to leave for several hours. So, Charlene, Andy, Bronson and the brothers all traipsed to the river.

"This is lovely," Charlene exhaled. "The air is so fresh."

"Yes, I love rivers. It's so peaceful."

Charlene laughed. "I wouldn't consider a picnic with two rambunctious boys very peaceful."

Bronson threw back his head and laughed.

Charlene sighed inside. She wasn't used to seeing any man's face or features clearly, but Bronson was very handsome.

"We better get back now." She rose reluctantly and called for the children to gather around.

The children's cheeks were flushed, which only assured her that bringing orphans West was a good thing. She especially loved seeing the glow on Andy's cheeks.

"That was fun," Andy's voice was full of excitement.

"Do we really have to leave

Bronson patted the boy on the back. "I'm glad you enjoyed yourself. This is what living in Kansas is like."

Andy's eyes lit up. "I'd like to live here then." He sought Charlene's face.

"I'd like to live here, too." She reached over and hugged him.

Bronson clasped his hands behind his back and walked away whistling.

CHAPTER TEN

From the train window, Cherryvale appeared on the horizon. Most of the buildings in the main part of town were made of bricks, which Bronson assured her were supplied by his brick factory.

"We've even begun to build roads with brick."

Both Charlene and Andy could barely hold back their excitement. Soon they would be in Cherryvale, and perhaps, if God blessed them, Charlene would find a job.

"What if you don't find a job before the train heads back to New York?" Andy asked.

"Bronson assured me we could stay in the hotel for a week. He will pay, and I can reimburse him once I get a job. I should be able to find something in a week."

"Especially now that you can see so well." Andy bounced up and down beside her.

Charlene's eyes fell on the heads of the two brothers. She lifted up a prayer that they would find a home together in Cherryvale.

As the train slowed, the Matron clapped her hands. Charlene asked the boys to stand. They were both very nervous. They held hands.

"Now don't worry. I'm sure there will be a home for you here." Bronson assured the boys. "We are a growing town. Remember, we even have a bicycle factory."

The boys' eyes lit. They couldn't wait to see the bicycles Bronson told them about, especially the "Ordinary" with a large front wheel and small wheel in back. The boys were led to a small church at the corner of the town. This time they reluctantly climbed up on stage. They refused to release one another's hand.

There were several families and a handful of farmers waiting to interview the children. When they saw how few children there were, several of them left without even speaking to Donald and Denver.

A farmer looked them over but shook his head because they were too small.

Charlene grew worried. She wondered if the boys would be adopted at all. The last family left the stage shaking their head. It was so obvious the boys would be miserable if parted, no one wanted to split them up.

Andy leaned over. "They're gonna have to go back to the orphanage."

Charlene slowly nodded her head. That meant she would have to return with them because she had agreed to help the Matron with the children the entire trip.

Suddenly, the door flew open and a rather peculiar looking man came through the door. He looked around the room until his eyes landed on the two boys. A huge grin spread across his face.

"There they are! Just the boys I've been looking for." The man pointed at Donald and Denver. The door opened again, and a lovely woman glided in. She caught up to the man. Once again, he pointed at the boys.

"There they are, Dora. Our sons! Didn't I tell you they would be here?"

The woman nodded up and down, tears beginning to fall on her cheeks. She rushed onto the stage, knelt in front of the boys then gathered them both in her arms.

Charlene didn't know what to say.

The man stepped forward and stuck his hand out to Bronson. "Good to see you, Jacobs."

"Glad to see you, too, Meyers." Bronson smiled.

Charlene stared at the man.

"Charlene, this is Jason Meyers and his wife."

Charlene allowed the man to shake her hand.

"We've come for the boys," Jason Meyers stated.

"But, how did you know…"

"God showed them to me in a dream. I've waited three years since that dream, but I knew today was the day. I had a hard time convincing my wife to come along, but you can see she's glad she did.

Bronson turned to Charlene. "Jason owns the bicycle factory. They live on a small farm just outside of town. The boys will have a wonderful life."

"I'm so glad," Charlene said and led them all over to the table to sign the adoption papers. Donald and Denver each held one of Mrs. Meyers' hands.

Charlene's eyes filled with tears as the small family left the building. "God was good to find homes for the children."

The Matron straightened her skirt with a grim smile. "I never doubted it. The Orphan Train has always been successful."

Charlene frowned. "I was told by Mr. McCully that sometimes children have to be returned to the orphanage."

"It's rare. We try not to bring too many children to assure they are all placed. I'll visit all these children in a year to make sure they are all happy."

"And if they aren't?"

"We try to find another placement for them. Miss Trumbel, it's the best we can do."

Charlene realized her tone of voice was rude. "I'm sorry. I know this is a wonderful program. I'm so glad you allowed me to come along. There is something I need to tell you."

"Can we discuss it on the train?"

"No, that's just it. I won't be returning to New York."

The woman's face registered shock.

"I've decided to stay here and try to get a job."

The older woman began to shake her head back and forth. "That will never do."

"I'm sorry, Matron, but I am an adult and can make my own decision."

"What about that boy?" She pointed at Andy.

"He will stay with me. Bronson assured us..."

The woman's head snapped up. "Bronson?"

"I mean... Mr. Jacobs..."

"So, that's what's going on. You've formed some kind of tender for that man. I must insist you come back to New York. It's not appropriate for a single woman..."

"No, Matron." Charlene held a hand up to stop the woman from speaking. "This has nothing to do with him. I believe I can get a job here, make a life for myself."

"What will your father say?"

"I'll telegraph him and explain everything."

The Matron stared at Charlene. "I think you're making a mistake, but I'll say no more. I'm sure if you have any problems, your father will send money to bring you home."

"Yes. I'm sure Father will send me some money right away. Andy and I will be staying in the hotel until I find a job and a place to live."

The Matron snorted, thanked Charlene for her help on the train, then turned and walked away. Charlene could see the disapproval in the way the woman carried herself.

Andy joined Charlene. "Matron doesn't look happy."

"No, she doesn't think we should stay in Cherryvale."

Andy kicked his foot. "Aw, does that mean we're going back to New York?"

She reached over and tousled his hair. "No. We are staying right here. I explained it all to the Matron. We are going to give it a try."

Andy jumped up and down then danced around and shouted, "Yahoo!"

Bronson stepped up beside them and clapped his hands together. "Well, are you ready to begin your new life? I'd love to show you around town, but first we need to get you settled into the hotel."

Charlene covered her mouth with her hand. "Oh, I forgot my suitcase on the train."

Bronson placed a firm hand on her wrist to stop her from running out of the room. "I took care of that already. Had it sent to the hotel."

Charlene sighed, "Thank you."

The three of them walked out of the church together.

The town was just as Bronson described. Most of the buildings were made from brick, and the town had begun work on streets from the same type brick.

"Oh, we have other factories, too."

"But the brick factory is the biggest one," Andy shouted as they walked down the street and stopped in front of the brick factory.

Charlene eyed Bronson. "You own the whole brick company?" She swallowed at the thought.

"Yes." His eyes locked with hers.

"You're very... wealthy then?"

He nodded.

Charlene bit her bottom lip and wondered why such a wealthy man would have anything to do with helping her. Yes, she came from a wealthy family as well, but he didn't know that. As far as he was concerned, she was just an old maid, who now wore spectacles.

"You've been so kind to me. How can I ever repay you?"

Lord, he's such a good man. Thank You for allowing him to help me.

A strange smile flit across Bronson's face. "You don't owe me anything. But once we get you settled in, I'd like to get to know you better. Perhaps I could entice you to go to dinner with me."

Charlene dropped her eyes. From his tone, she understood he meant more than a friendly dinner. She was surprised. A man like Bronson could court any woman he wanted. Why did he seem interested in her?

"I'm sure that would be lovely. However, you don't need to do anymore for me. Once I get settled, it's my responsibility to find a job and make a life for Andy and myself."

Bronson reached out and pushed a strand of hair, which had fallen loose from the bun Charlene wore, back behind her ear. Her flesh tingled where his hand brushed it.

"But I want to help you. We are friends, are we not?"

Charlene straightened. "Yes."

"Then, please, allow me to continue to help you. But my dinner invitation would not be part of that. I'm asking if I can start courting you."

Charlene's mouth opened, but no words came out. Finally, she was able to whisper, "You want to court me?"

Bronson nodded and pulled her closer to him.

"But... but... I'm an old maid."

Bronson threw back his head and laughed. "How old are you?"

"Twenty-four." Her lips trembled.

"I'm thirty. If anyone here is old, it's me."

"But why would you be interested in me? I'm clumsy and cannot see well."

"We fixed all of that with spectacles, although I found the way you bumped into things rather charming."

"Y...yes. But you wouldn't want to be seen with me wearing the spectacles."

Bronson cocked his head. "Why ever not?"

"They make me look..." her voice trailed away.

"As far as I am concerned, they change nothing. You are a beautiful woman, inside and out. Your spectacles only enhance the beauty of your eyes."

Charlene's hand fluttered to her chest. She was sure her heart was about to burst from her chest.

Could it be true, Lord? Could a man like Bronson actually find her attractive, with her spectacles?

"I see I will have to prove my feelings to you." Bronson took another step closer, placed a hand under her chin then gently tilted her head until she was looking up at him.

He stared down into her eyes, spectacles and all.

"I'm in love with you, Charlene."

He lowered his head and pressed his lips against hers.

A MONTH LATER: CHAPTER ELEVEN

Charlene sat at the desk and finished typing the article: *Orphan Train Riders*. First, she would show it to her boss, the editor of the *Cherryvale Bugle*. Next, she would mail it to a New York newspaper. She could only hope it would someday be printed there.

Just then, the front door of the small brick house near Main Street flew open, and Andy ran in.

"The boss told me to ask you if you were ready to go on that picnic?" The boy's voice was bright and happy.

Andy was thriving in Kansas and worked part time at the brick factory with Bronson. The other half of the day, he had a private tutor who was helping him catch up so he could attend school the following year.

Charlene stood and stretched. "Yes, I just finished my article about the Orphan Train."

Andy stopped. "I want to hear it."

"I'll read it to you and Bronson during the picnic!" She laughed and shooed him from the room. "Grab the basket off the counter."

Within an hour, they were all happily walking together beside a small river, enjoying the fresh air.

"I think your article is one of the most well written and informative pieces I have ever heard," Bronson said, admiring the pink hue that flushed Charlene's cheeks.

"Yes, if it gets published, I believe it may help raise funding for the continuation of the Orphan Train. I only wish there was more I could do."

Bronson stopped, sat down and pulled Charlene beside him. Andy scampered off, searching for insects.

"There is more you can do." Bronson leaned over and stuck a small flower behind her ear.

"What?"

"You could adopt children from the Orphan Trains."

"That would be lovely. However, I can't afford any more children. My salary at the *Bugle* is just enough for Andy and me. Without your help, we couldn't even make it."

"Yes, but I can afford the children."

Charlene turned wide eyes toward Bronson. "What... what are you saying?"

"I'm not saying anything. I'm asking."

Charlene reached up to take her spectacles off. Bronson brushed her hand aside.

"No, Dear, I want you to see me when I ask you this. Charlene Trumbel, would you make me the happiest man alive by marrying me?"

A small tear formed in the corner of her eye. Charlene couldn't believe this was happening. A dream come true.

"But, Bronson, are you sure? What will people say about you marrying a woman who wears..."

Bronson stopped the flow of words with a gentle kiss.

"I love you, Charlene. I want to marry you, just as you are. We can adopt a whole house full of Orphan Train riders."

Charlene bent her head and leaned against his chest. "Yes, Bronson, I will marry you."

"Do you love me, Charlene?" Bronson asked.

"Yes, with all my heart."

Bronson stood, pulled her to her feet, then bent his head and swept her away in a passionate kiss. When he finally let her go, Charlene's head was spinning with joy.

Bronson leaned over and pressed small kisses onto the tips of Charlene's glasses.

Charlene smiled at him.

"You're sure about wanting to marry me? And adopting Andy, too?"

Bronson nodded. "I can hardly wait."

Charlene leaned in and whispered. "God has given me everything I've ever dreamed of."

Bronson smiled and pulled her into a warm embrace. "Ours will be a happy life, Darling. It will be a true spectacle of love."

TERESA IVES LILLY

Teresa Ives Lilly loves to write Christian Fiction. In general, she writes novella length romance, but has been known to write a mystery or two and full-length novels.

Her novel, "Orphan Train Bride" quickly went to number one on Amazon's best seller list and stayed in the top ten for two weeks when first published.

She has participated in many novella collections which have also been on the Amazon's best seller list.

Teresa would love to hear from her readers. Readers can follow Teresa at www.teresalilly.wordpress.com

Teresa is always thankful for positive reviews left on Amazon for her books.

Teresa resides in San Antonio, Texas

www.ingramcontent.com/pod-product-compliance
Lightning Source LLC
LaVergne TN
LVHW090607030225
802813LV00009B/450